...n's fur was dark brown and stripy all over,
...ad enormous green eyes. As Megan
...he bent down to lick something that was
...his paws.

..."s Cosmo," Tess told Megan. "He's really
...d friendly. He's been looking after that toy
...er since he got here!" Megan tiptoed over
...down next to him. She reached out
...d stroked the top of his head. His fur was
...ismo gave a rumbling purr and bumped
...igainst Megan's hand to get more and
...ntion.

...Megan cried. Cosmo rolled onto his back
...y batted Megan's hand with his paws.
...:ked up the little toy mouse that he'd
...ing and dangled it for him to play with.
...d up and took it in his mouth, then
...o onto Megan's lap and started pawing at
...iaking it nice and comfy before he put
...-toy down. Megan stroked his fur all the
...to his tail, and Cosmo arched his back
...another purr that made her hand vibrate.
...n't want to move in case she scared
...him, but she wished she could give him a big hug.
He was the most adorable thing ever!

www.kidsatrandomhouse.co.uk

Have you read all these books in the Battersea Dogs & Cats Home series?

🐾 🐾 🐾 🐾

COSMO'S
story

by
Sarah Hawkins

Illustrated by Artful Doodlers
Puzzle illustrations by Jason Chapman

RED FOX

BATTERSEA DOGS & CATS HOME: COSMO'S STORY
A RED FOX BOOK 978 1 849 41411 1

First published in Great Britain by Red Fox,
an imprint of Random House Children's Books
A Random House Group Company

This edition published 2011

1 3 5 7 9 10 8 6 4 2

The Random House Group Limited supports the Forest Stewardship Council
(FSC), the leading international forest certification organization. All our titles
that are printed on Greenpeace-approved FSC-certified paper carry the FSC
logo. Our paper procurement policy can be found at
www.randomhouse.co.uk/environment.

Mixed Sources
Product group from well-managed
forests and other controlled sources
www.fsc.org Cert no. TT-COC-002139
© 1996 Forest Stewardship Council
FSC

Set in 13/20 Stone Informal

Red Fox Books are published by Random House Children's Books,
61–63 Uxbridge Road, London W5 5SA

www.**kids**at**randomhouse**.co.uk
www.**totallyrandombooks**.co.uk

Addresses for companies within The Random House Group Limited
can be found at: www.randomhouse.co.uk/offices.htm

THE RANDOM HOUSE GROUP Limited Reg. No. 954009

A CIP catalogue record for this book is available from the British Library.

Printed and bound in Great Britain by
CPI Bookmarque, Croydon, CR0 4TD

Turn to page 93 for lots
of information on the
Battersea Dogs & Cats Home,
plus some cool activities!

❧ ❧ ❧ ❧

Meet the stars of the Battersea Dogs & Cats Home series to date . . .

Bailey

Misty

Chester

Rusty

Max

Daisy

Snowy

Stella

Huey

Angel

Cosmo

The Birthday Surprise

"I asked her again and again and AGAIN," Megan Hobbs said dramatically. "But Mum STILL wouldn't tell me what my birthday surprise is."

Megan's best friend Amy sighed in frustration. "At least you're going to find out tonight," she said, linking arms with Megan as they walked round the play ground. "It would be soooooo annoying if you had to wait two weeks until your actual birthday."

Megan nodded. "Waiting this whole afternoon is bad enough – I just want to know what it is! Maybe Mum and Dad are taking me to Disneyland!" she joked. "And they'll pick me up from school in a private jet."

"No, a pink limousine!" Amy giggled

"OOH yes, a pink limousine. And they'll tell me that I'm really a princess and I never have to go to school again!"

Both girls giggled as they added more
and more exciting details to the birthday
surprise. By the time their friend Maria
came over, Megan was getting her own
palace and a herd of
flying unicorns!

"What's so
funny?" Maria
asked.

"We're just
trying to
work out
what Megan's
mum and dad
are getting her
for her birthday,"
Amy explained.

"Well, I know what the best present
in the world would be!" Maria said,
waving a piece of paper at them.

"Look!"

Megan and Amy crowded round to look at the photo. It was a picture of Maria's ginger cat, Marmalade. Curled up next to her were five tiny orange kittens! "They're so small they can fit on my hand!" Maria squealed. "They don't even have their eyes open yet."

"That's it!" Amy gasped, glancing up at Megan. "Your parents are going to give you one of Marmalade's kittens!"

Megan shook her head sadly. Having a kitten would be better than getting a trip to Disneyland *and* a pink limo, but it would never happen. "Mum says I'm not old enough to look after a pet," she sighed. "I don't think she'll ever change her mind."

Megan stared at the picture of the baby kittens longingly. One of them had their mouth open in a tiny kitten yawn. "They're sooo cute. You're so lucky, Maria."

"You can come and play with them as soon as they're big enough," Maria promised. "They can be your royal lions," she said grandly, making Megan and Amy laugh again.

When the school bell went at the end of the day, Megan waved goodbye to her friends and rushed over to the place where her mum usually waited in the car. Mum waved at Megan through the windscreen as she got closer – but there was someone in the front seat

next to her – a man with short brown
hair and square glasses.

"Dad!" Megan squealed as she opened
the car door. "What are you doing here?"
Her dad had a long journey to work, and
he never got home before Megan finished
school. "Are *you* my birthday surprise?"

"No!" Dad laughed as she climbed into
the back, next to Becca's car
seat. Megan kissed her
baby sister on her
chubby cheek,
and Becca
gurgled in
delight. "We're
going to go and
choose it now."

"But what
is it?" Megan
burst out.

Mum laughed. "Shall we tell her?" she asked Dad.

"Go on, then," he smiled. Mum and Dad turned round in their seats so they were facing Megan. Mum looked as excited as Megan felt!

"Since you're going to be eight," Mum said with a big grin, "Dad and I think that you're old enough to look after a pet. What do you think? Would you like to have a cat for your birthday?"

Megan squealed so loudly that Dad
had to put his hands over his ears.

"I think that's a yes," he joked.

Battersea Dogs & Cats Home

Megan gasped. Amy had been right! For once she couldn't think of a thing to say. She just sat there with her mouth wide-open. A cat of her very own – it was like a dream come true!

Mum and Dad laughed at her shocked face. "What do you think then, Meg?" Dad asked.

"Yes PLEASE!" she shrieked. "I can't believe it! OOOOHHHH!" She squeezed her sister in excitement. "I'm getting a cat, Becca! He can be yours too, though," she said generously. "What do cats say? *Miaow!*"

"Mee-wow," Becca copied.

"Good girl, Becca!" Mum said. "And thank you, Megan, for being so kind.

You're going to have to be a really good big sister and show Becca how to play with it nicely."

"Are we going to get one of Marmalade's kittens?" Megan asked.

"Who's Marmalade?" Dad was puzzled.

"Maria's cat. She had kittens the other day. Maria showed me a picture. They were so tiny and so sweet, and their eyes weren't even open yet!" Megan curled up in her seat to do an impression of the tiny yawning kitten.

"Well, they sound lovely, but we're going to go to Battersea Dogs and Cats Home,"

Dad told her. "They look after all kinds of cats and dogs that don't have anywhere nice to live. We can give one of those cats a good home and make sure that it has a happy life."

"A boy in my class got his dog from Battersea," Megan said, "but I didn't know they had cats there.  Aren't they scared of the dogs?"

Mum laughed. "They don't all live together. The cats have their own bit of Battersea, called a cattery. There are lots of cats there, so I'm sure we'll find the perfect one for you."

"We won't be able to bring it home with us today, though," Dad explained.

"Someone from Battersea will have to come round and check our house first, to make sure it's a nice place for a cat to live. But we can go there now and choose it, and then we should get it in time for your birthday."

Megan squealed again. Earlier on today she thought she'd never be allowed a cat, and now here she was about to go and pick one of her very own! "What are we waiting for?" she exclaimed. "Let's go!"

On the way to Battersea Megan taught Becca everything she knew about cats. "You're not allowed to pull their tails," she said sternly, "but you can stroke them nicely and they purr like this:" Megan made a purring noise and rubbed her head against Becca's car seat.

Becca tried to copy her, but ended up blowing a raspberry. Megan giggled.

*

When they arrived, Megan was so excited she could barely stand still while Mum strapped Becca in her buggy.

"I'm glad you're happy, Meg," Dad laughed, "but you're going to have to calm down a bit. You'll scare all the animals if you keep jumping about!"

Megan took a deep breath and managed to walk normally – but she couldn't stop smiling!

They went into reception and were met by a friendly lady called Tess.

"I don't think I need to ask who's getting a pet," she joked. Megan's grin grew even bigger.

"Do you know what type of cat you're looking for?" Tess asked her. "Longhair or shorthair; a cat or a kitten?"

As Tess said *kitten*, Megan caught her breath and turned to her mum and dad. "Oh, a kitten! *Please* can we get a tiny little baby kitten?"

Megan's mum smiled. "Kittens need more work than grown-up cats, love.

They need more attention and more care, just like human babies. We'd have to house-train it, and you'd have to play with it every day . . ."

"I will, I *promise*. Cross my heart," Megan said, looking up earnestly at her parents. "I'll play with it every morning before school, and after school, and all weekend long. And Becca can play with it while I'm at school. She'd be a big sister as well then, just like me. *Please?*"

Mum and Dad smiled at each other. "Have you got any kittens at the moment?" Dad asked Tess.

Megan shrieked and squeezed Dad around the middle as tightly as she could. "Oh thank you, thank you, thank you!" she squealed.

"As a matter of fact, we do!" Tess told them. "We've got a new litter that will be ready to be re-homed soon. They were left on our doorstep in a box when they were just a few weeks old."

Megan gasped. She couldn't imagine why anyone wouldn't want to keep kittens, but at least Battersea had been there to look after them until they found homes of their own. And she was determined to give one of them the best home ever – with her!

After their chat Tess led them up a spiral staircase. As Megan got to the top, she let out a squeal of excitement. There were glass doors all around her, and behind each one was a different cat!

As they walked in, some of the cats came over to the glass to say hello. Megan held Becca's hand and read out each cat's name as they rushed from pen to pen. There was a huge white longhair Persian called Bruce, a black-and-white cat named Pearl, who was sitting on top of a scratching post, and a fat orange tabby called Tiger who peered up at them . . .

But there weren't any kittens.

Suddenly Tess stopped at a large door in the corner of the room.

"Here they are," she smiled.

Megan and Becca raced over and looked in. There, all curled up together in a basket, were the most beautiful kittens Megan had ever seen!

Meeting Cosmo

Megan stared at the four tiny kittens in the cage. They were even cuter than Marmalade's babies!

"Remember, they're still very little," Tess said as she unlocked it. "Don't go in too fast or you'll scare them."

Mum picked up Becca and they all crept into the pen. "Look, Becca, cats." Mum said softly.

"Tat," Becca repeated, pointing her chubby finger at them.

Megan crept into the cage, holding out her hand to the tiny kittens. They were all stripy tabbies, but they had different markings. One with a white patch on its nose rushed right over and pounced at Megan's feet playfully, making her giggle. Tess threw a jingly ball and two of the other kittens chased after it. Megan bent to stroke one of them as they went past.

Mum put Becca down beside Megan.

"That's Apollo and that's Zeus," Tess told her. "They're both a bit naughty! The one with the white nose is a girl, she's called Cupid." Tess picked up Cupid and gave her to Megan for a cuddle.

"Won't they miss each other, though?" Megan asked, looking at Mum and Dad worriedly. "It would be horrible if I had to live somewhere away from Becca."

"We can't look after four cats, love," Mum told her, "and I'm sure they'll all find nice homes."

"They'll be fine," Tess said reassuringly. "You'll just have to give your kitten lots of love and attention to make up for it!"

Megan looked down at the tiny animal squirming in her arms. They were all lovely – but Megan wasn't sure that any of them were *her* kitten. She put Cupid down and looked round the pen. Mum, Dad and Tess were watching Apollo and Zeus tumble over each other, but Becca was staring at the basket – and a tiny kitten was staring back at her!

His fur was dark brown and stripy all over, and he had enormous green eyes. As Megan watched, he bent down to lick something that was between his paws.

"That's Cosmo," Tess told Megan. "He's really gentle and friendly. He's been looking after that toy mouse ever since he got here!" Megan tiptoed over and knelt down next to him. She reached out slowly and stroked the top of his head. His fur was so soft!

Cosmo gave a rumbling purr and bumped his head against Megan's hand to get more and more attention.

"Oh!"
Megan
cried.
Cosmo
rolled onto
his back
and gently
batted her
hand with
his paws.
Megan picked up the little toy mouse that
he'd been holding and dangled it for him
to play with. He reached up and took it
in his mouth, then jumped up onto
Megan's lap and started pawing at her
skirt, making it nice and comfy before he
put the mouse- toy down. Megan stroked
his fur all the way down to his tail, and
Cosmo arched his back and gave another
purr that made her hand vibrate.

Megan didn't want to move in case she scared him, but she wished she could give him a big hug. He was the most adorable thing ever!

Dad bent down next to her and tickled Cosmo under the chin. "Oh, he's lovely, isn't he? Look, Becca."

Mum reached down so that Becca could touch Cosmo's soft fur. Becca reached out and Cosmo sniffed her hand and then gave her finger a little lick. "Tat, tat!" Becca gurgled.

"Well it looks like he'd be nice and gentle with Becca," Mum said, "but it's up to you, Megan."

Cosmo turned around in a circle and snuggled down on Megan's lap. Then he looked up at her with his big green eyes. *Mew*, he said hopefully.

Megan looked down at him and felt like she was going to burst into tears. She was just so happy! "He's the one I want," she said to her mum and dad. "I think I love him already!"

Cosmo started purring again. He dropped the toy mouse between his paws and nuzzled it with his little pink nose.

"I think we're going to have to have a pet mouse too!" Mum laughed.

Cosmo Comes Home

Sure enough, when Dad came home two weeks later with a pet carrier, the toy mouse was in there with Cosmo!

"Megan! Jo! Becca!" Dad called as he came in the front door. Megan let out a squeal and dashed down the stairs, jumping over the last steps. The previous two weeks had gone really slowly – she just couldn't wait for Cosmo to arrive.

A few days after they'd met Cosmo, a lady from Battersea had come round and checked that their house would be a nice home for a kitten. Dad had put a cat flap in the back door, but the lady told them that they'd need to keep it locked for a while, because it wouldn't be safe for Cosmo to go outside until he'd had all his injections and grown up a bit. Other than that, she'd said that she was sure the little cat would be very happy with them.

Since then it seemed like mum had been bringing home toys for Cosmo nearly every evening – it was like it was nearly *his* birthday, not Megan's!

Dad put the pet carrier on the kitchen floor, next to the cat-litter tray that Megan had got all ready for Cosmo's arrival. There was a towel covering the bars of the carrier door so that Cosmo didn't get upset by the journey. Megan carefully pulled it off and gazed at the tiny ball of fluff inside. Even now he was here she still couldn't believe that she really had her very own kitten.

Cosmo trotted up to the bars and sniffed her fingers, then rubbed his head against her hand. "Looks like he remembers you!" Mum said.

"Welcome home, Cosmo!" Megan smiled. "Can I get him out, Mum?"

"Just open the door and we'll let him come closer in his own time," Mum told her.

Megan undid the latch and swung open the door, then crouched down next to the carrier. Mum and Dad sat on the floor next to her, with Becca on Mum's lap, and they all watched the open doorway.

For a while Cosmo stayed out of sight at the back of the carrier, and Megan and her family waited patiently.

Just as Megan's bum was starting to go numb from sitting on the floor, a paw appeared!

Cosmo cautiously put one tiny paw out onto the kitchen floor, and then another, and then he poked his face out and meowed hello!

Once he was out of the carrier, Cosmo looked around at everything curiously, his tiny tail flicking from side to side. He came and rubbed up against Megan, but didn't want to sit on her lap. There was too much to explore! He stalked all about the kitchen, sniffing every corner, rubbing against the kitchen cupboards and pawing at the doors. He even squeezed into the gap between the washing machine and the cupboards.

As she watched the tiny kitten disappear, Megan started to worry, and gave her dad a panicky look.

"Don't worry!" Dad laughed, "he got in, so he can get out again. Show him his mousie, I'm sure he'll come out then."

Megan crawled over to the pet carrier and brought the mouse-toy out. "Cosmo!" she called, waving the mouse in front of the gap. At once Cosmo bounded from the small space and took the toy in his mouth, then he wandered across the kitchen like a mummy cat carrying a kitten. "Phew!" Megan sighed happily.

When the washing machine started making a loud whirr, Cosmo crouched down and meowed at it loudly, his head moving in circles as he tried to follow the clothes as they whirled around.

Everyone laughed, waking up Becca, who had fallen asleep on Mum's lap. She gave a loud wail. "Oh, I think someone's hungry," Mum said, getting up with a sigh and popping Becca in her high chair. "Let's give Cosmo some dinner as well. Do you want to do it, Megan?"

"Yes please!" Megan cried. She pulled a chair over to the kitchen cupboard and knelt on it to get a tin of cat food out.

Cosmo must have recognized what it was because he meowed very loudly and hungrily! Megan got down and Cosmo rubbed against her legs, weaving between her feet as she walked across the room to spoon it into his bowl.

"Careful, Cosmo, you're going to trip me up!" Megan laughed. "Shall I give him some milk, Mum?" "Go on then," Mum said. "But he can't have it that often. Everyone thinks cats drink milk all the time, but really they should only have it as a special treat."

"It's like you having ice cream," Dad added. "It wouldn't be good for you to have it every day!"

Megan got the bottle out of the fridge and carefully poured some into Cosmo's drinking bowl.

Mew, Cosmo purred happily as he sniffed at the milk. Then he patted it with his paw!

"Oh, Cosmo!" Megan laughed, but the little kitten didn't seem to mind having damp toes. Pointing his leg out delicately like a ballet dancer, he licked his paw clean with his small pink tongue.

Once Cosmo had finished, Megan
picked him up for a cuddle. He snuggled
into her shoulder and gave her neck a
lick. Megan giggled as his rough tongue
tickled her skin. "Cosmo!" she protested,
"I've already had a wash this morning!"
She didn't complain too much, though.
It was so nice to be covered in kitten
kisses, even if they were a bit wet!

Bird-watching

Megan spent the rest of the afternoon following Cosmo around the house and giggling as he explored. He was fascinated by everything! As soon as something moved he'd jump at it, whether it was the living-room curtains or Dad's feet!

After Cosmo had pounced on Dad's slippers and attacked his newspaper,

Dad put down the paper
and gave Megan a
very stern look.

"Come on,
Cosmo," Megan said,
picking him up carefully,
"we'll find you a toy of your own to play
with." She took her kitten into the lounge
to find the cat toys Mum had bought him.
When he saw the scratching post, Cosmo
started to wiggle and Megan let him jump
down and rub against it. Megan picked
up one of his new toys – a stick, with
purple feathers dangling from a long
string. She held it so
that the feathers
touched the top
of the scratching
post and jiggled
it up and down.

As soon as Cosmo saw the movement
of the coloured feathers he stood
completely still and his eyes grew even
bigger than normal. Without taking his
eyes from the feathers he sank low to the
floor, then with a spring of his back legs
he jumped up onto the post. Before
Megan had time to move
the stick he had the
feathers trapped
between his
paws!

"Good boy, Cosmo!" Megan laughed. Then she reached down to move the feathers away from him – Maria's cat always ruined her toys by chewing and attacking them. But instead of biting and clawing like Marmalade did, Cosmo was gently licking the feathers clean!

When Megan finally got the feathers away from Cosmo, she ran off with them, holding the stick so that they trailed behind her for Cosmo to chase.

He raced
after her and kept
trying to jump on
them, but then suddenly he
stopped still in front of the
patio doors that led out into the
garden. At first Megan wondered if
he'd caught sight of his own refection
and thought it was another cat, but then
she saw a bird fly up
into the oak tree
just outside.
Cosmo's head
moved as he
followed the bird's
journey, and he let
out a little *miaow*.

"Remember, he's not allowed to go outside yet!" Mum called. "We don't want to lose him."

"I know, he's just watching the birds."

"Oh yes," Mum walked over to the window with Becca balanced on her hip. "Look, Becca, there's a birdie! It looks like a blue tit, oh, and look – there's a nest!" She pointed to a spot in the old oak tree. Megan could just make out a bundle of twigs on one of the branches. There were two blue tits taking it in turns to fly in and out of it.

"It looks like they might be taking food to their baby chicks," Mum told Megan. Every time one of the birds fluttered past the window

Cosmo paced up and down and pawed at the glass. He looked at Megan and made a pleading mewing sound.

"You can't go out there," Megan told him, picking him up and giving him a hug. Cosmo snuggled into her arms, but he didn't take his eyes away from the birds flying outside, just out of reach.

"It's probably a good thing Cosmo can't go out," Dad told Megan as he came over to tickle the stripy kitten under his chin. "It's in a cat's nature to hunt, and I bet he thinks those blue tits would make a good snack,"

"He wouldn't," Megan said crossly.

"Cats are meant to hunt mice too and Cosmo just cleans his toy mousie!"

"It does seem like he's a big softie!" Mum agreed.

"That's what makes him so special," Megan said, giving him a cuddle.

Presents and Pouncing

That evening Megan and her mum sat on the sofa to watch TV – or they tried to! At first Cosmo was fascinated by the flickering screen and sat in front of it as if he was watching it too, but then he got bored and started to paw at Megan's legs.

Megan patted the seat and he jumped up next to her, but instead of sitting down, the curious cat climbed all over them. Then he stood on Mum's legs and sniffed under the cushions. Megan stroked his back, but just when it looked like he was going to settle down for a cuddle Cosmo scrabbled up onto the back of the sofa!

"What are you doing, you funny kitten?" Megan giggled, turning round and kneeling on her seat to make sure Cosmo didn't fall. Cosmo stalked along the back of the sofa like he was walking a tightrope.

"The TV is this way," Mum joked.

"Playing with Cosmo is more fun than watching any TV programme." Megan smiled, stroking his tiny paws.

Cosmo looked down at his paws, then bent to lick her fingers. He turned in a circle on her lap, pawed at her legs to make a comfortable spot and then curled up in a ball. Megan stroked his soft fur, tracing the pattern of his stripes. As Cosmo started to purr, Megan felt like the luckiest girl in the world. She looked up and saw Mum watching her with a happy smile. "I love him so much," she whispered.

Mum smiled. "He is beautiful. He feels like part of the family already, and you've looked after him really well today. So, you like your birthday surprise then?"

Megan gasped. "I'd forgotten! I'd actually forgotten it's my birthday tomorrow!" she cried, making Cosmo jump.

"Shhhh!" Mum laughed.

Megan giggled. "Oops. Don't want to wake up the best birthday present ever!"

The next morning Megan woke up to some singing. But wasn't coming from her radio alarm clock – it was Mum and Dad standing in her bedroom doorway with their arms full of presents! "Happy Birthday, dear Megan," they sang, "Happy Birthday to you!"

"Morning, Mum!" Megan said as she jumped out of bed. "Morning, Dad," she cried as she rushed past them out of her bedroom.

"Where's Cosmo!" Megan could hear her parents laughing as she ran down the stairs and burst into the lounge.

Cosmo was already awake and was curled up in his basket with his toy mouse. "It's my birthday, Cosmo!" Megan yelled, throwing herself down next to his basket and scratching him behind the ears.

He gave a big lazy cat stretch and rolled onto his back so that Megan could stroke his tummy while he purred louder and louder.

"Ahem!" came a noise from the doorway. "Shall we throw these presents away then?" Dad joked.

"No!" Megan shrieked, jumping up and flinging her arms round her parents and kissing Becca on the cheek. "I'm just SO happy! It's my birthday AND Cosmo's here! It's the best day of my whole entire life!"

When everyone was settled in the lounge
Megan started opening her first present.
Cosmo's ears pricked up at the sound of
the rustling paper, and when Megan took
out the jewellery box and threw the
wrapping paper to one side Cosmo
climbed over her legs and pounced on it!
Megan burst into laughter as her kitten
peered out from underneath the paper
and gave a curious
Meow?

After that Megan was more interested
in the wrapping paper than the presents!
As she opened each one she scrunched
the wrapping into a little ball. Every time
the paper crackled Cosmo crouched low,
his ears flat against his head, and when
Megan threw it he scampered
after it, batting it
around with
his paws.

Becca loved watching him and giggled, "Tat, tat, tat," over and over again.

"Now I know why he liked my newspaper so much!" Dad laughed, looking down at the baby cat, who was now patting a piece of bubble wrap with his paw.

"Be careful, Cosmo, that's not normal paper . . ." Mum warned him.

But it was too late, Cosmo stepped onto the bubble wrap – and jumped when it made a loud *pop*! He shot behind Megan and she picked him up, stroking him gently.

"You scaredy-cat!" she laughed.

Meow, Cosmo said, snuggling up to her happily.

After every present was unwrapped and the paper was in little balls all over the lounge floor, Megan gave Cosmo a bit of ribbon to play with. "Now you're ready for the party too, Cosmo!" she said happily.

Party Time!

After she'd opened all her presents, Mum
told Megan to go upstairs and get dressed.
"If you don't hurry up all your friends will
arrive for your party and you'll still be in
your pyjamas!" she said with a smile.

"Come on, Cosmo!" Megan dragged a
piece of wrapping paper after her and
Cosmo followed her, jumping on it as he
went.

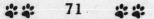

Megan put on her
pink velvet dress.
It was really soft
and nice to
stroke, but not
as nice as
Cosmo's
beautiful
tabby fur! She
had just pulled
on her tights –
managing to stop
Cosmo from
laddering them with his claws – when the
doorbell rang.

"Megan, hold on to Cosmo," Mum
called from downstairs as she opened
the front door. Megan picked Cosmo up
so that he wouldn't try and go outside,
and ran down to meet her friends.

It was Amy, wearing a blue dress, with blue ribbons in her dark hair.

"Ahhhhh!" Amy exclaimed when she saw Cosmo. "He's so tiny!"

"Isn't he gorgeous?" Megan said proudly. When Poppy, Maria and Olivia arrived, all of them fussed and cooed over Cosmo as well.

Megan felt so happy as she told them all how sweet he was with his little toy mousie. "He takes care of it like it's *his* pet!" she laughed.

As if he'd heard her, Cosmo trotted over with the mouse in his mouth. He sat down with it between his paws, and started to lick it all over.

Then, as Megan and her friends watched, he nudged it towards Megan with his nose, looked up at her with his enormous blue eyes, and gave a little *miaow*.

"Look, Cosmo's giving you a birthday present too!" Amy gasped. "That is sooooo adorable!"

"Oh, Cosmo!" Megan cried, "but you love your mousie." Cosmo rubbed his head against her legs and purred softly. *I love you more*, he seemed to say.

All of Megan's friends wanted to play with Cosmo. They were so distracted by making him chase after the wrapping-paper balls that Mum had to call them three times to get them to go into the kitchen for Megan's birthday lunch.

Everyone *oohed* again when they saw all the food laid out on the table. There were loads of crisps and biscuits, and triangular sandwiches full of ham and cheese.

Megan tore a little bit of ham out of her sandwich and fed it to Cosmo, who nibbled it gently, being careful not to bite her fingers.

"He's the sweetest cat I've ever seen," Amy declared.

"Marmalade's lovely too," Megan said quickly so that Maria's feelings weren't hurt.

Maria smiled. "You should all talk to your mums," she said to Amy, Poppy and Olivia. "If we each have kittens we could have a kitten club!"

The girls tucked into the birthday meal, talking excitedly about kitten club and taking it in turns to have Cosmo on their laps.

Cosmo was sitting quietly on Megan's lap, purring as she stroked him, when suddenly he gave a loud *miaow* and jumped down. As the girls watched he started pacing about by the patio doors, and then rushed from them to Megan's chair and back again.

Megan tried to pick him up but he jumped down again and started winding round the legs of her chair and miaowing louder than before. "Do you want some food too?" Megan asked him. She got up and went over to fill up his bowl.

"Megan, he wants to go out," Poppy called.

"No!" Megan shouted, but before she could move, Poppy opened the door . . . and Cosmo ran out into the garden.

Little Cat Lost

"No!" Megan shouted. "He can't go out yet, he's too little!" She burst into tears. "Mum! Cosmo's outside!" Then she pushed past Poppy and into the garden. "Cosmo!" she called, her voice heavy with tears. "Cosmo!"

Mew, came a reply. A sob caught in Megan's throat and she turned to see Cosmo sitting underneath the big oak tree, next to the patio doors. Megan sobbed again – with happiness this time. She stepped over to the little kitten and quickly picked him up. "Oh, Cosmo, I thought I'd lost you," she cried into his fur.

Mum burst out of the kitchen looking as pale and panicky as Megan felt. "Oh, thank goodness!" she cried. Then she turned and shouted indoors, "Don't worry, it's OK, Megan's got him."

She rushed over and gave Megan and Cosmo a big hug. "It's OK," she murmured over and over again. "You've had a fright but Cosmo's fine. Let's go back inside, Poppy's very upset – she didn't know Cosmo wasn't allowed out."

But Cosmo was scrabbling round in Megan's arms, mewing sadly. He kept trying to get back to the tree. Megan and her mum looked over at the tree trunk. There was something small at its base, close to where Cosmo had been sitting, and as they watched, it moved. Still holding Cosmo tightly, Megan went to look. It was a tiny baby bird! "Mum look!" she cried. "It must have fallen out of its nest, that's why Cosmo wanted to come out here!"

Mum bent down
and gently
picked up the
little bird.
"It's not
hurt at all!"
she said in
surprise.
"Any other
cat would
have tried to
eat it, but
Cosmo must have
been looking after it!"

Carefully, Megan's mum stood on an
upturned flowerpot and put the baby bird
safely back into the nest. "The adults
might get scared and abandon the nest if
they think someone has been near it,"
she explained.

Megan carried Cosmo inside, where a tearful Poppy was being comforted by the others. "I'm so, so, so sorry," she sniffled. "Is Cosmo OK?"

"Yes," Megan said kindly, knowing that Poppy was feeling really bad. "He wanted to go outside so he could save that little bird. If you hadn't let him out it might have died."

"Cosmo's a hero!" Amy smiled.

"Girls, come and look," Mum said. She was standing at the patio doors. Megan and her friends crowded round, and they watched as the mother bird swooped down. She perched on a branch close to the nest and hopped along it, putting her head on one side to try and work out if something was wrong.

Megan held her breath, hoping that the mummy bird would go in and feed her chicks. Suddenly, with a flutter of wings, the bird disappeared into the nest.

Everyone cheered, and Cosmo joined in with a loud *Miaow*. Megan gave him a proud pat.

"Phew!" said Megan's mum. "Well, that was an adventure!

Especially for you, Cosmo," she said as she stroked his soft head.

"I think it's time for some birthday cake," she cried, "and a special fishy treat for Cosmo!"

"Cosmo, the kindest kitten in the world!" Megan said proudly.

Read on for lots more . . .

🐾 🐾 🐾 🐾

Battersea Dogs & Cats Home

Battersea Dogs & Cats Home is a charity that aims never to turn away a dog or cat in need of our help. We reunite lost dogs and cats with their owners; when we can't do this, we care for them until new homes can be found for them; and we educate the public about responsible pet ownership. Every year the Home takes in around 12,000 dogs and cats. In addition to the site in southwest London, the Home also has two other centres based at Old Windsor, Berkshire, and Brands Hatch, Kent.

The original site in Holloway

History

The Temporary Home for Lost and Starving Dogs was originally opened in a stable yard in Holloway in 1860 by Mary Tealby after she found a starving puppy in the street. There was no one to look after him, so she took him home and nursed him back to health. She was so worried about the other dogs wandering the streets that she opened the Temporary Home for Lost and Starving Dogs. The Home was established to help to look after them all and find them new owners.

Sadly Mary Tealby died in 1865, aged sixty-four, and little more is known about her, but her good work was continued. In 1871 the Home moved to its present site in Battersea, and was renamed the Dogs' Home Battersea.

Some important dates for the Home:

1883 – Battersea start taking in cats.

1914 – 100 sledge dogs are housed at the Hackbridge site, in preparation for Ernest Shackleton's second Antarctic expedition.

1956 – Queen Elizabeth II becomes patron of the Home.

2004 – Red the Lurcher's night-time antics become world famous when he is caught on camera regularly escaping from his kennel and liberating his canine chums for midnight feasts.

2007 – The BBC broadcast *Animal Rescue Live* from the Home for three weeks from mid-July to early August.

Amy Watson

Amy Watson has been working at Battersea Dogs & Cats Home for six years and has been the Home's Education Officer for two and a half years. Amy's role means that she organizes all the school visits to the Home for children aged sixteen and under, and regularly visits schools around Battersea's three sites to teach children how to behave and stay safe around dogs and cats, and all about responsible dog and cat ownership. She also regularly features on the Battersea website – www.battersea.org.uk – giving tips and advice on how to train your dog or cat under the "Amy's Answers" section.

On most school visits Amy can take a dog with her, so she is normally accompanied by her beautiful ex-Battersea dog, Hattie. Hattie has been living with Amy for just over a year and really enjoys meeting new children and helping Amy with her work.

The process for re-homing a dog or a cat

When a lost dog or cat arrives, Battersea's Lost Dogs & Cats Line works hard to try to find the animal's owners. If, after seven days, they have not been able to reunite them, the search for a new home can begin.

The Home works hard to find caring, permanent new homes for all the lost and unwanted dogs and cats.

Dogs and cats have their own characters and so staff at the Home will spend time getting to know every dog and cat. This helps decide the type of home the dog or cat needs.

There are five stages of the re-homing process at Battersea Dogs & Cats Home. Battersea's re-homing team wants to find

you the perfect pet, sometimes this can
take a while, so please be patient while
we search for your new friend!

Have a look at our website:
**http://www.battersea.org.uk/dogs/
rehoming/index.html** for more details!

"Did you know?" questions about dogs and cats

- Puppies do not open their eyes until they are about two weeks old.

- According to *Guinness World Records*, the smallest living dog is a long-haired Chihuahua called Danka Kordak from Slovakia, who is 13.8cm tall and 18.8cm long.

- Dalmatians, with all those cute black spots, are actually born white.

- The greyhound is the fastest dog on earth. They can reach speeds of up to 45 miles per hour.

- The first living creature sent into space was a female dog named Laika.

- Cats spend 15% of their day grooming themselves and a massive 70% of their day sleeping.

- Cats see six times better in the dark than we do.

- A cat's tail helps it to balance when it is on the move – especially when it is jumping.

- The cat, giraffe and camel are the only animals that walk by moving both their left feet, then both their right feet, when walking.

Dos and Don'ts of looking after dogs and cats

Dogs dos and don'ts

DO

- Be gentle and quiet around dogs at all times – treat them how you would like to be treated.
- Have respect for dogs.

DON'T

- Sneak up on a dog – you could scare them.
- Tease a dog – it's not fair.
- Stare at a dog – dogs can find this scary.
- Disturb a dog who is sleeping or eating.

- Assume a dog wants to play with you. Just like you, sometimes they may want to be left alone.
- Approach a dog who is without an owner as you won't know if the dog is friendly or not.

Cats dos and don'ts

DO
- Be gentle and quiet around cats at all times.
- Have respect for cats.
- Let a cat approach you in their own time.

DON'T
- Never stare at a cat as they can find this intimidating.

- Tease a cat – it's not fair.
- Disturb a sleeping or eating cat
  – they may not want attention
  or to play.
- Assume a cat will always want
  to play. Like you, sometimes
  they want to be left alone.

Some fun pet-themed puzzles!

What a cat needs!

Here is a list of things that a cat needs for a long, happy and healthy life. See if you can find them in the word search and while you look, think why they might be so important. The words could be written backwards, diagonally, forwards, up and down so look carefully and GOOD LUCK!

M	D	F	G	T	R	E	Z	D	F	S	F	A	S	P	D	Q	F	R	N
H	T	O	Y	S	H	D	J	K	U	O	E	W	V	C	B	N	U
F	A	U	H	D	C	J	N	V	N	M	B	F	O	X	Q	A	Y	G	L
Y	G	E	Q	J	F	R	D	G	R	K	H	B	F	D	E	F	G	R	T
C	F	R	S	T	Y	P	A	K	T	J	U	T	F	E	H	S	O	A
R	U	I	M	N	L	I	T	T	E	R	T	R	A	Y	D	R	C	O	Q
O	G	R	D	S	G	T	E	D	C	X	V	R	H	F	S	R	G	M	V
K	C	O	L	L	A	R	P	J	K	H	A	E	F	T	G	N	T	I	H
P	O	U	G	R	F	D	G	T	E	F	I	K	H	G	F	B	V	N	C
L	W	Q	D	G	A	N	J	B	R	G	B	N	N	D	H	D	E	G	U
X	J	V	E	T	C	A	R	E	U	G	D	R	G	W	Q	H	K	L	U
B	S	F	H	J	U	R	C	D	G	E	S	F	T	P	H	T	D	G	W
J	L	U	G	D	R	B	U	I	B	F	L	Z	V	T	O	K	I	H	K
K	F	T	W	E	F	Y	G	J	U	Y	R	O	P	G	X	S	J	M	F
M	I	C	R	O	C	H	I	P	K	I	O	D	V	S	F	D	T	N	Z
J	K	U	F	D	J	B	C	S	L	I	J	A	Z	E	O	L	C	X	R
Q	W	D	G	K	B	X	F	T	Z	A	L	G	N	M	D	C	V	T	E
F	G	H	U	O	K	V	D	E	W	S	Y	E	J	S	T	A	E	R	T
K	L	H	F	B	U	R	D	G	U	E	A	F	H	Y	R	F	E	N	A
E	R	E	S	P	O	N	S	I	B	L	E	O	W	N	E	R	S	I	W

FOOD
SCRATCHING POST
MICROCHIP
WATER
LITTER TRAY
TREATS
COLLAR
TOYS
TAG
PLAY
BED
VET CARE
LOVE
GROOMING
RESPONSIBLE OWNERS

Remember: a cat needs the litter in its tray change at least once a day.

Can you think of any other things a cat may need? Write them in the spaces below.

Cat Breeds Crossword

Across

1 These orange and black coloured cats are nearly always female. (13)

3 These spotted cats are the result of breeding with wild cats and share their name with a type of tiger. (6)

4 Brown cat with black stripes. (5)

7 A blue eyed oriental cat with a white body and colour on its head and tail. (7)

9 Like the siamese but all one colour and shares its name with people who come from Burma. (7)

10 This colour of cat can be deaf and may need sun cream on its ears on hot days. (5)

11 This breed of cat has no tail and comes from the Isle of Man. (4)

12 A type of persian that shares its name with a pet rodent with thick fur. (10)

13 This breed has no fur at all and shares its name with a statue in Egypt. (6)

Down

2 This cat is always trying to catch Tweety Pie. (9)

4 This cat is always getting beaten up by a mouse called Jerry. (3)

5 These grey coloured cats have thick fur and come from England. (7,4)

6 The name of the Blue Peter cat. (6)

8 A long haired breed that needs lots of grooming. (7)

9 The colour of cats that witches have and at Battersea they often find it harder to get homes because of their colour. (5)

Transform these white cats by adding some colour. You could turn them into one of the breeds from the crossword or make them look like your own cats or cats that you know.

HAPPY COLOURING!

Remember: grooming plays a big part in building a bond between you and your cat.

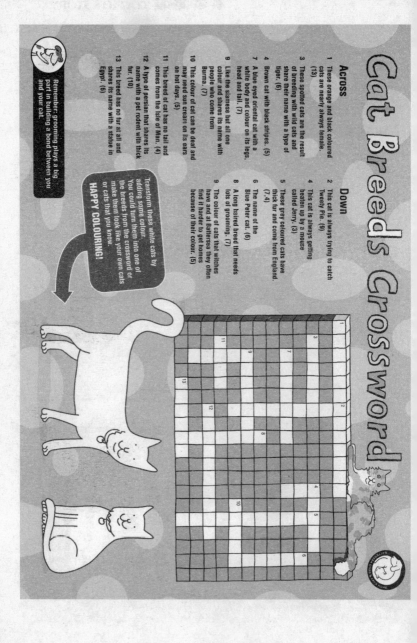

108

Fingerprint dogs and cats.

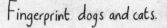

Thumb print over corner of scrap paper and remove to leave white triangle for nose and mouth.

Stick-on eyes: Hole-punched pieces of paper with dots marked in the centres.

Or use white paint to make eyes and tummy.

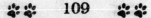

Here is a delicious recipe for you to follow.

Remember to ask an adult to help you.

Cheddar Cheese Cat Cookies

You will need:

227g grated Cheddar cheese

(use at room temperature)

114g margarine

1 egg

1 clove of garlic (crushed)

172g wholewheat flour

30g wheatgerm

1 teaspoon salt

30ml milk

Preheat the oven to 375°F/190°C/gas mark 5.

Cream the cheese and margarine together.

When smooth, add the egg and garlic and mix well. Add the flour, wheatgerm and salt. Mix well until a dough forms. Add the milk and mix again.

Chill the mixture in the fridge for one hour.

Roll the dough onto a floured surface until it is about 4cm thick. Use cookie cutters to cut out shapes.

Bake on an ungreased baking tray for 15–18 minutes.

Cool to room temperature and store in an airtight container in the fridge.

BATTERSEA DOGS & CATS HOME

There are lots of fun things on the website, including an online quiz, e-cards, colouring sheets and recipes for making dog and cat treats.

www.battersea.org.uk